PAGETURNERS® | SCIENCE FICTION

ESCAPE from EARTH

JANICE GREENE

PAGETURNERS®

SADDLEBACK
EDUCATIONAL PUBLISHING
www.sdlback.com

ISBN-13: 978-1-68021-394-2
ISBN-10: 1-68021-394-6
eBook: 978-1-63078-795-0

Printed in Malaysia

21 20 19 18 17   1 2 3 4 5

3 1327 00684 2280

Chapter 1

I take pride in the fact that I'm smart about people. With one look, I can tell whether a person is going to be cool or a jerk. Take my father, for example. His droopy eyes and mouth tell you that the guy's a loser, a quitter. It was obvious that he was the type to leave his family. My mom should have seen it coming.

So when I first met my college roommate, I was really disappointed. His name was Darryl. He had beady little eyes and thin lips. I thought he was self-centered and sneaky. And probably a creep. But that wasn't even half the story.

Darryl stood at the door to our student apartment. He had a gym bag in one hand.

And a large backpack was slung over one shoulder. He brought the bag inside and set it down.

"Here. Let me help you with that backpack," I said.

"No!" he shouted.

"Okay, okay." I backed off.

"My name is Darryl," he said.

"I'm Nick." I reached out to shake his hand, but he just looked at me.

"I'm glad to be with you. You are a safe person," he finally said.

A safe person? What an odd thing to say.

"Where are you from?" I asked.

"Russia," he said.

"You're a long way from home. Is Darryl your real name?" I asked.

"You wouldn't be able to pronounce my real name," he said. Then he smiled at me. "I am glad we are going to the same university."

I'd like it better if I had another

roommate. But then I thought about my mom. "Give people a chance," she says. So I asked him if he wanted to get something to eat. But Darryl said he wasn't hungry. That was fine with me.

Earlier that day, I'd met a nice guy named Mike. We're both studying computer animation. Maybe I'd run into him.

That night I had a weird dream. Darryl had this strange contraption. It was made up of wires and tubes. He was speaking into it, using some strange language. It didn't sound like Russian to me.

It was the next morning. Darryl was gone before I woke up. He must have had an early class. I was thinking how nice it was to have the place to myself. That's when there was a knock on the door. It was a girl. The first thing that caught my eye was her long, bronzed legs. She also had a wide forehead, which I associate with being honest. Her eyes were a deep, warm brown. I knew she was someone special.

"I'm Kara," she said. "I'm from the apartment building across the way. Would you mind if I came in for a few minutes? I need to borrow your window."

"The window?" I asked as she came in and walked past me. "Sure. Come right on in," I said sarcastically.

She set down a bag full of tools. "I'm just going to drill a hole in the wall of the building outside your window. Is that okay? I'm setting up a clothesline," she said.

"Is that allowed?" I asked.

"Sure," she said. "It's part of living green. The school encourages students to line-dry their clothes rather than use an excess of energy."

I wasn't sure I believed her. "You're not from around here, are you?" I asked.

"No. I'm from Arizona," she said. "Why?"

"That explains your nice tan, plus the fact that you're totally insane." I laughed. "I can't imagine putting up a clothesline in the foggiest city in the country. It'll take your clothes a month to dry. But what the heck. It's still a great idea."

"Why would you say that if you don't think it'll work?" she asked.

"Because without the clothesline, you never would have knocked on my door. And now we can get to know each other."

"Wow! You don't waste any time," she said with a smile. She had a great smile.

Kara showed me how the clothesline device worked. There were two plastic casings that held either end of a cable. A casing would be mounted to the building outside each of our windows. First we mounted the casing on my side.

"Now I just have to do the same thing on my side," she said.

"How are you going to get the cable from one building to the other?"

"I'll hold one end and toss the other end to you," she said. "The buildings aren't that far apart. It's only about fifteen feet."

"Have you got a good arm? It's three stories down if you miss," I said.

"I won't miss," she said confidently. Then she went to her apartment.

A few minutes later, I saw her open her window and wave. "Ready?" she called out.

"Ready," I said.

Then she tossed her end of the cable, and it sailed through my window. In fact, it landed right in my hands. "Perfect," I called out to her.

"Of course," she said. Then she came back to my apartment.

"Now, that's a clothesline," I said. "We should celebrate. Let's see. I have bottled water and ..." I looked around. "And granola bars," I said as I grabbed a box off the kitchen table.

"Don't you have some studying to do?" Kara asked with a grin.

"Yeah. But it can wait," I said. "Right now I want to know everything about you. Your major. What you like to do for fun. And most important, why you came all the way to San Francisco for school."

At that moment Darryl came in. When he saw Kara there, he looked alarmed. Then he turned to me. "She must leave here. She is not a safe person," he said in a low voice.

"Are you out of your mind?" I said.

"Excuse me?" Kara said to Darryl.

"Please," Darryl insisted. He looked like he was about to panic.

"Take it easy," I told him. "Maybe you're the one who needs to leave." What a jerk. I was going to throw him out. But when I grabbed his shoulder, a shock ran through my fingers and up my arm. "Ow!" I yelled.

"What did he do?" Kara asked.

Darryl gave me a pitiful, pleading look. In a few moments the pain had faded from my hand and arm. I stared at him, wondering if I'd imagined the shock. "Let's get out of here," I said to Kara.

We went to her apartment.

"Why did you let that guy push you around?" Kara asked.

"I felt sorry for him," I said.

"I think he might be unstable," Kara said. "You should think about getting a new roommate."

"Maybe I should give him a chance," I said. "I don't really know him yet."

She leaned closer to me. "If you wait, he might do something even crazier," she said.

"You might be right," I said.

By the time I got back to my apartment, I'd decided to take Kara's advice. I would call student housing and ask for another roommate. But Darryl seemed to be reading my mind. I hadn't been there five minutes when he begged me to let him stay.

"I'm sorry to make you miserable," he said. "But please don't make me go. I will have to be leaving soon anyway."

He looked so anxious and sad that I felt myself giving in. "Really? Why?" I asked.

"I have family problems," he said. He stood up and grabbed his backpack. "I have to go now. I'll see you later."

It was nice having the place to myself all morning. I called Kara and asked her if she wanted to hang out tomorrow. She was such a cool girl. I knew we'd have a lot of fun together.

I was just starting my homework when there was a knock on the door. There were two serious-looking guys in suits. They looked like brothers.

"We're campus security," one of them said. "We're looking for Darryl."

While he was talking, the other guy went over to Darryl's bag. "One of the professors is missing some important papers," he said. "They're in a black backpack. Have you seen anything like that around here?"

Chapter 2

So Darryl was a thief. I have to admit I was surprised. Sure, the guy was a little weird. But a criminal? I was about to tell the guy what I knew about Darryl. That's when I glanced over at the other guy. He'd made a long slit in Darryl's bag. Now he was pulling something out of it. There was a satisfied grin on his face. I could hardly believe my eyes. It was the strange contraption Darryl was using when I thought I'd been dreaming.

But what was with these guys? They shouldn't be trashing Darryl's stuff. It wasn't right. "Hey! You guys aren't security!" I yelled. "Get out of here before I call the police." I grabbed my phone off the desk.

One of the guys stepped behind me

and threw his arm across my chest. His grip was like iron. Then something hard pressed against my neck. And sharp pains shot through me like knives. I wanted to scream, but I couldn't even open my mouth. I couldn't move either. My legs turned to jelly. But the guy's iron-like arm held me up.

"Tell me everything you know about Darryl and the backpack," he said. "Then I'll let you go."

I was in too much pain to speak. Suddenly, Darryl was there. He looked at the guy holding the contraption, then moved quickly toward him. The guy stepped backward and dropped it. There was the sound of breaking glass as it hit the floor.

Darryl pulled something out of his jacket. It was a short tube. He held up his other arm. His watch was glowing with a bright light. Then he held the tube in front of it. In a split second, a beam shot out of the tube toward the guy's stomach. The hot ray of light covered him in what looked like a cocoon. Then the floor seemed to rise up in front of me. And suddenly everything went black. When I opened my eyes, I had a terrible headache. Spots danced in front of my eyes.

Darryl helped me up off the floor. "Nick," he said. "Are you going to be all right?" His face looked concerned and sincerely sympathetic.

"I'm about half-blind. But otherwise I'm okay," I said. The pain had gone. And the spots were slowly fading away.

Now there was an awful odor in the room. "What's that smell?" I asked.

Darryl pointed. On the floor were scraps of charred clothing and tiny bits of shoes and a belt.

"Is the guy—" I started to say.

"He is destroyed," Darryl said. "But the other one escaped."

I couldn't believe it. Darryl actually

killed the guy. "Why are they after you?" I asked.

Darryl sat on the bed. The backpack was in his lap. "I wanted to keep you out of this. But that will no longer be possible. Nick, I'm not … from here. The men you saw? They are my enemies," he said. "They blew up my planet in the last space war. Families were killed. Everything was ripped to shreds and scattered in space. Only a few of us escaped before the final moment. And now I have a treasure to guard. Look."

He opened the backpack, and I looked inside. It felt as though I might fall forward into the deep cloud of swirling colors. As I looked through the shades of green, blue, and yellow, I could see tiny eyes. There seemed to be thousands of them. Feeling dizzy, I looked up at Darryl.

"They are ready to grow," he said as he closed the backpack. "When they do, there will be enough for my planet to be created again. But in a new place."

"You risked your own people's future to save me," I said.

"Those men would have killed you for no good reason," he said.

"But now the one guy knows where you are," I said. "You're still in danger."

He nodded. "I must leave. I need a safe place to hide until my friends come for me," he said.

"I'll help you," I said. "I grew up in San Francisco. There's no part of this city that I don't know about."

Darryl looked at me for a few seconds. His fingers moved nervously over the straps of the backpack.

"Tonight I must be at Point Reyes. Can you help me get there?" he asked.

"Yes. But we'll need a car," I said. I thought about it. My mom worked across the bay. It would take her an hour to get here. Then I thought of Mike, the guy I met yesterday. He had a car. I was sure he'd let me borrow it. "Stay here," I told Darryl. "I'll be back as soon as I can."

The expression on Darryl's face was trusting and hopeful. I suddenly felt a huge weight on my shoulders. This was a big responsibility. And if I failed ...

I hurried to Mike's apartment. I knocked on the door, but no one answered. I'd have to try back a little later.

Then I thought about Kara. She was smart and resourceful. And she could definitely help with this mission. Luckily, she was alone when I knocked on her door. She opened it and smiled.

"Couldn't stand to be away from me for a whole hour, huh?" she said.

"Kara. Listen to me. Something amazing has happened. And I want you to help me," I said. What else could I do? I told her everything. About the strange visitors. The fight. And Darryl's backpack. I watched her face as I spoke. She looked shocked when I told her about Darryl killing one of his enemies. But she didn't say anything. She just kept staring at me with a serious expression on her face.

"You believe me, don't you?" I asked when I'd finished.

"Yes," she said.

"I knew it. I knew I could count on you." I grabbed her by the shoulders and kissed her.

"I need you to go with me to Point Reyes," I explained. "I'm going to check with a friend about borrowing his car. Then we'll hide out for a few hours before we leave. Meet me in my room in about fifteen minutes. And bring some food and warm clothes." She nodded.

When I got back to my apartment, I could see that Darryl was upset. "You told her," he said.

"It's okay. I'm smart about people," I said. "Believe me. We can trust Kara."

At that moment I heard a knock. I opened the door. It was Kara. She glanced at Darryl nervously. Then she took my hand and pulled me outside.

"I like you, Nick," she said. "You're a really nice person. Now, I want you to understand that what I've done is for your own good. You need serious help. And you need it right now.

"I've called the police. They're coming to talk to you. They'll be able to help. And they're going to put Darryl where he won't pose a danger to other people."

Chapter 3

I covered my face with my hands so Kara wouldn't see my shock and anger. Then after a moment I said, "You're right." I took deep, loud breaths. It gave me time to think. Then, before Kara knew what was happening, I quickly backed into my room and locked the door.

She started pounding on the door. "Nick! Let me in!" she yelled. "Do you hear me? Let me in!"

I ran to the window and opened it. "Darryl," I whispered. "Grab your backpack and a belt. Then watch what I do. You're going to do the same thing." I took off my belt and climbed up onto the windowsill.

I tossed the belt over the clothesline and gripped it with both hands.

Darryl looked confused, but he nodded and watched.

I stepped off the windowsill, still gripping the belt. And I immediately started to move. The window to Kara's apartment was just a little lower than mine. So the downward angle made it easy to glide across. When Kara's window was just inches away, I twisted my body away from the wall and jumped to the ground.

I looked up at my window. Darryl was on the windowsill. I could see his backpack over one shoulder. And his belt was slung over the clothesline. He looked ready to go. "Don't look down," I called out.

But then he looked down. After a few seconds of hesitation, he grabbed the ends of the belt and took off along the clothesline. He was heading straight for the opposite wall. At the last second, he twisted his body away from the building. But before he could jump, his shoulder rammed into the wall.

That's when I heard a strange kind of whistle. It was coming from Darryl. I thought it must be a sound of pain. Then he dropped to the ground. I ran over to him to see if he was okay. He was breathing hard and rubbing his shoulder. "That was fearsome," he said.

"I told you not to look."

"Where can we hide?" Darryl asked.

"I'm thinking of a place downtown."

"Will we take the bus?" he said.

"Yes. But not the one that's near here. They'll be looking for us there. Come on," I told him.

We went to the back of the apartment complex and walked along the alleyway. There was a chain-link fence at the end. We climbed it and landed in the parking lot on the other side. I could see signs on the buildings. KEEP OUT! DANGER! The place seemed deserted. Then I heard a low, menacing growl behind us. The dog wasn't huge, but he was muscular. He seemed to have no neck at all. The animal walked slowly toward us.

"Why is it threatening us?" Darryl asked calmly.

"He's been trained to guard this area," I explained.

"Okay," said Darryl. He slowly reached into his pocket.

"Okay?" I said. I picked up a stick that was lying on the ground and waved it at the angry dog.

With a snarl, the dog leaped at me. He grabbed the stick with his mouth. From the corner of my eye, I could see that Darryl was holding the tube he'd used yesterday. Then the dog let go of the stick and leaped toward me again. This time he knocked me to the ground. The next thing I knew his paws were pushing down on my chest. It felt like a heavy lead weight. I could feel his hot breath on my face.

Suddenly a beam of bright, hot light shot out. It just missed the dog's ear. The surprised animal yelped and ran away.

Still shaking with fear, I got to my feet. "That's what you did to that guy yesterday," I said. "How does it work?"

"When you capture light from another source, the tube channels the rays into power," he said.

"Do your enemies have tubes like that?" I asked.

"No," he said. "Their weapons are more deadly."

More deadly than dead?

Darryl was breathing heavily by the time we reached a wooded area. It was thick with trees and shrubs. We worked our way over fallen branches and tangled vines. Darryl tripped several times.

Finally we reached the mall. "Okay, we'll hide in there for a while," I said, pointing to the large building.

"But that place will be packed with people," Darryl said.

"That's the point. It's hard to spot someone in a crowd," I said. "We'll hide your backpack in a shopping bag."

Darryl looked worried. "Nick," he said. "Your judgment has not exactly been perfect so far."

"Oh yeah?" I said. "Wasn't that clothesline a great way to escape?"

"But what about your friend Kara?" he asked, shaking his head. "You are wrong about people."

"Just her. But even if I was wrong about her, I'm right about this. Or do you have a better idea?" I asked.

"We can hide in the woods until nighttime," he suggested.

"You can sit in the cold, drippy trees for hours," I said. "But I'm starving."

"You are not a waiting person," Darryl said. "But you have clever ways to break free. I'll come with you."

I felt guilty. Hiding in the woods was probably a good plan. I should have followed Darryl's suggestion. After all, he was the one with so much at stake. But the thought of staring at tree trunks for hours made me a little crazy.

The mall was pretty full. People were out of school and off work. At the food court, I waited in line to get a burrito. "Don't you ever eat?" I asked Darryl.

Darryl's beady little eyes sparkled. "Oh yes, Nick. I'm eating now," he said with a smile.

"What?" I said, staring at him. Darryl was just standing there. Nothing was going into his mouth but air.

"Our bodies absorb food in a different way. It goes through a special patch we wear under our clothes," Darryl said. "Would you like to see it?"

Normally I'm a curious person, but I said no. All I could think about was my own empty stomach. I was half-finished with my burrito when a cop walked by. He didn't seem to notice us, but just the sight of him made me nervous. "Let's go," I said.

"I thought you said we would be hidden in the crowd, Nick. Why are you so restless?" Darryl asked, looking worried.

"It's that guy in blue," I said. "He's a cop. A police officer."

We took the escalator to the ground floor. On the way down, we passed another cop. As we got off the escalator, I saw dozens of adults and kids sitting around a fountain. There was a cop here too.

"Wait a minute," I said to Darryl. I

looked around and counted three more cops on the ground floor. Two more were leaning over the second-floor railing. They were looking directly at us.

Chapter 4

Darryl was no fool. He figured out what was happening right away. "They want to capture us," he said. Before I could say a word, he pulled the tube from his pocket.

His hand moved so fast I couldn't tell where he was aiming. Then beams of light shot out in three directions. The water in the big fountain was suddenly boiling, sending up a blinding cloud of steam. People started screaming as they jumped off the benches and pulled their kids away.

At the same time, the front window of a video store buckled from the heat. It collapsed in about a million pieces of glass. Shoppers shrieked and were backing away just as a potted tree behind us caught fire. And all of this happened in about three seconds.

The entire mall erupted in chaos. All around us, parents were yelling. They were frantically trying to get their kids to safety. Other shoppers were shouting and running, even knocking people down in their mad rush toward the exits. A few people tried to help calm the crowd.

I saw one cop stand up on the bench surrounding the fountain. His eyes were focused directly on Darryl. But then we were swept away in a wave of people. The next time I looked, a cop was waving everyone toward the rear exit. "This way!" he shouted. "That's right. Keep moving."

We blended into the crowd and left the building. A lot of people were headed for the bus stop.

"The cops will be watching the buses

around here," I said. "Let's walk for a while." This was my chance to show Darryl that I could be patient.

We'd been walking through the streets for about ten minutes. Everything was quiet. Then we heard sirens coming from the direction of the mall.

"What is this place you want to go to next?" Darryl asked.

"It's an electronics plant," I said. "It's where they make computers and the parts that go into digital devices. My dad used to work there."

"And he no longer works there?" Darryl asked.

"No. He got fired after he and my mom broke up," I said.

Darryl looked confused. "Could you explain *fired* and *broke up*?" he asked.

"Sure. *Fired* means he was doing a bad job, so they made him leave. *Broke up* means that he and my mother aren't together anymore," I said.

"I'm sorry. That is a sad thing for all of you," Darryl said kindly.

"My father ran out on us," I said. "I don't care if I ever see him again."

After an hour of walking, I figured it was safe for us to get onto a bus. By now, it was late afternoon. And the bus was half-empty. A few teenagers were heading home from the mall. And there were some tired-looking parents holding kids and shopping bags.

I couldn't believe it. Just a few hours earlier, I was a guy with homework to do. And I had a date with Kara to look forward to. Now that seemed like a year ago.

There was a faint buzzing in the air. A tiny insect passed behind Darryl's neck. He turned and made a low whistling noise. His eyes were wide. "It's a spy device," he whispered. "Can you hit the bug with water?"

"Water? I don't have any," I said.

Darryl quickly reached over to a girl sitting across the aisle. He grabbed her water bottle. "Excuse me," he said. "My friend will pay you for your water."

"Hey!" the girl shouted. "What are you doing? Give that back to me."

Darryl began squirting streams of water at the bug. "I keep missing it. Help me, Nick," he said.

"What do you think you're doing?" a large man demanded.

In the seat ahead of me was a mother with a small child and a baby. She was feeding the baby. There was a bottle in the baby's mouth. I grabbed it out of the mother's hands. "Sorry, I need this," I said. The baby started to cry.

I squeezed the bottle hard, squirting milk everywhere but on the bug.

"You idiot," the mother said. Then she

handed the baby to her older child and stood up. The woman was a lot bigger than me.

"You're getting me wet," an old man sitting across the aisle said to me.

"What's going on back there?" the bus driver shouted.

"It's a deadly mosquito!" I yelled. "We've got to kill it!"

The woman with the children put her hands together and clapped them next to Darryl's ear. Then she cried out in pain. She opened her hands, swearing. The tiny gray pest was stuck in one palm. And her hand was rapidly turning red.

Darryl poured water over her palm. Then he picked off the bug and carefully and dropped it into his shirt pocket. The mom scowled at him. "Jerk," she said.

The brakes squealed as the bus came to a stop. The driver walked back toward us. "All right," she said, sounding annoyed. "What's all the commotion?"

Darryl and I ran toward the exit, but the large man stepped out and blocked our way. "You're not going anywhere," he said.

I didn't know what to do. That's when I realized that I was still holding the baby bottle. So I squirted his face with a stream of milk.

"You little punk!" he yelled, grabbing for me. I saw Darryl put his hand on the man's shoulder. The man suddenly stopped. His eyes were wide. I knew that Darryl had shocked him. It was just like he'd done to me.

I ran for the doors and pushed them open. Darryl was right behind me. I jumped to the curb and Darryl followed. We ran across the street and kept running until we were far from the bus. Both of us were panting heavily. We stopped to catch our breath.

"I thought humans were made up of mostly water," Darryl said after a while. "Why didn't you use your own supply?"

I had to think about it for a second. "It's not something that we're adapted to do," I said.

"That's too bad," he said.

"It's okay, Darryl. That's not how we normally defend ourselves," I said. "Now let's see that spy thing."

He pulled the flying bug out of his pocket and gently placed it in his palm. The object was very tiny. It was about the size of a grain of rice. I held it closer to get a better view. It was a gray cylinder with one glassy eye.

"That's the recording part of the device," Darryl said. "They know where we are."

Chapter 5

If they know where we are, we should hurry," I said. Luckily, we were close to the electronics plant. It was in the industrial part of downtown. There was very little traffic. Only employees of the businesses came and went. That's why I thought we might be safe.

It took us about ten minutes to get to the main building. We walked through the parking lot, past all the trucks. The security guard station was just ahead. We'd have to check in.

"Hi," I said to the guard, smiling politely. "I'm here to see the shipping supervisor. Chuck Gunnison?"

"Your name, please?" she asked.

"I'm Nick Fuente," I said.

She looked more closely at me. "I recognize that name," she said with a smile. "Your father is Richard Fuente. He's such a nice man."

A nice man? She must have been thinking of someone else. And why was she talking about Dad like he still worked here?

"Chuck should be in shipping. But you might have to check in production," she said.

"Chuck knows all the drivers," I told Darryl as we walked away. "He'll get us a ride to Point Reyes."

I led Darryl down a hallway. There were offices on one side. On the other side was a glass wall. "What is this place?" Darryl asked.

"These are offices of the workers," I said, motioning to the closed doors. "There are engineers who design the products. And the computer technicians develop software."

Darryl was looking through the glass. "What's in there?" he asked.

"This is where the production workers put the products together," I said. "Some people connect the parts. And others test the devices to make sure they work right."

"Why do the workers wear those outfits?" Darryl asked.

"Those are called bunny suits. They keep dust and other particles out of this area. It has to be clean. In fact, they call this a clean room," I said. Then I looked around. The place had really changed since I was a little kid. "Look over there," I told Darryl. "Those machines are putting parts together."

Next we walked to the shipping department. "After the products are packaged, they come here," I explained to him. "Then they're shipped out to customers."

I walked up to a worker. "Is Chuck around?" I asked.

"He just went to production," the man said. "He should be back in a minute."

I didn't want to wait, so we headed back to production. But before we could leave the area, a machine was quietly gliding in Darryl's direction. He looked at it with a curious look on his face.

"It's a mobile robot," I told him. "Technically, it's an Automatic Guided Vehicle. AGV for short. It's controlled by electric wires in the floor. It picks up products from the racks and takes them to the conveyor belts for shipping."

That's when I saw him. It was Dad.

"Nick." He was walking quickly over to us. But then he stopped. "I thought that was you," he said. We stared at each other.

"You're all grown up," he said.

"Yeah," I said. "What are you doing here? I thought you got fired."

"This is your father?" Darryl asked.

I nodded.

"We can't stay here, Nick," Darryl whispered. "They'll find us. Believe me. They search every connection."

"Okay, we'll go," I said.

For once, my dad actually seemed to be concerned about me. "What's going on, Nick? Are you in some kind of trouble?" he asked. Then he looked at Darryl suspiciously, as if he was waiting for an explanation.

Darryl ignored him. "Hold out your hand," he said to me.

I did as he said. Being careful not to touch me, Darryl dropped something into my hand. It was a metallic container about the size of a pack of gum.

"If the backpack is destroyed, take this to the lighthouse at Point Reyes tonight," Darryl said. "My friends will take it from you."

"What is that?" Dad asked as I put the container into my pocket.

"It's none of your business," I said.

"I'm still your father, Nick."

"Look, Dad. I came here to see Chuck, not you. Darryl and I are leaving now."

Just then a man came running up to my dad. He had a frightened look on his face.

"Mr. Fuente," he said. The man was out of breath. "Some strange guys came to the guard station a few minutes ago. The guard tried to stop them." He shook his head. "I think she's dead."

"Dead? What do you mean?" Dad asked. "Where are these guys now?"

Darryl and I looked at each other. We'd seen them at the same time. The guys were standing just inside the door. There were four of them. They all looked like brothers. But I was beginning to understand that they weren't human. They were aliens. And they were Darryl's enemies. One of them held what looked like a steel pole. It was the length of a baseball bat.

A security guard came running toward

them. He was holding his gun in the air. "Hold it right there!" he shouted.

The alien with the pole pointed it at the guard. A blast of blinding white light shot out. Instantly the guard was gone, along with a blackened chunk of the concrete floor.

People were running and yelling as they ducked behind equipment. An AGV carrying a steel barrel collided with a forklift that had been left unattended. That impact sent the barrel crashing to the ground. It rolled directly toward the aliens, knocking one of them off his feet. But he quickly got back up. The aliens were intent on finding Darryl.

From the corner of my eye, I saw Darryl run up a conveyor belt that wasn't operating. He grabbed the tube from his pocket and held it up. But it was too late. The aliens had seen him.

The alien with the weapon turned toward Darryl and aimed at him. But instead of hitting Darryl, he hit the power button of a belt full of moving packages. The button instantly melted, and the conveyor belt came to a stop. But the packages continued to move at high speed, flying off everywhere.

Darryl continued walking up the belt he was on. Then the alien aimed his weapon and hit the rollers at Darryl's heels. Darryl lost his balance and fell down through the gap. A worker went over to where he'd fallen and was helping him up. That's when one of the aliens grabbed the worker. Another alien held his weapon to the back of the man's head.

Darryl slowly lowered the tube, and two of the aliens pulled him away from the conveyor belt. One grabbed the backpack from Darryl's hand. Then all four aliens walked him toward the door to the loading dock. He turned and gave me a desperate look I'll never forget. The look said, "Help me. Please."

As the aliens reached the door, the one

with the weapon turned and looked quickly around the room. Then he stared up at the ceiling. It was as if he were studying it. He slowly raised the tip of the weapon.

"Run!" I yelled.

Streaks of light shot toward the beams on the ceiling. Then, from out of nowhere, Dad appeared and grabbed my arm. "This way!" he yelled. We ran toward the loading dock.

Screams and shouts rang out behind us. Then I could hear terrible cracking and tearing sounds. The roof beams were beginning to collapse. There was a deep rumble as the ceiling started to shift and break apart.

Inside the loading dock, I saw Darryl's tube lying on the ground. I pulled away from Dad and grabbed it. The door to outside was only a few steps away. Just then a chunk of wood and plaster hit the floor next to me and broke apart. It barely missed me. I made it to the big bay door and jumped to the ground below. The door to the nearest truck was unlocked. And the keys were in the ignition. I got inside and put the tube on the seat beside me. I'd just started the engine when my dad opened the passenger door and got in.

"What are you doing?" he asked.

"Leave me alone," I said. I tried to shove him away. But he grabbed my arm and held it tightly. I had forgotten how strong he was.

"You're not going to Point Reyes," Dad said.

Chapter 6

I pulled loose from Dad's grip and started driving. "I *am* going," I said calmly. He looked like he wanted to say something, but he kept quiet.

People were now running through the parking lot. Many appeared to be injured. One man was carrying a woman with a bloody leg. I had to drive slowly to avoid hitting someone.

Then there was a loud rolling boom. I stopped and looked out the back window. The entire roof of the electronics plant was folding inward. Within seconds, the building caved in on itself, creating a billowing cloud of dust.

Once I made it to the street, I stopped. "Okay, Dad," I said. "You can get out here."

"No," he said.

"You should stay here and help," I told him.

"I'm staying with you," he said.

"Since when?" I said. "You haven't been there for me the past three years."

We drove across town in silence. Finally, we left the city and crossed the Golden Gate Bridge. Dense fog made the lights between the towers a fuzzy orange color. I glanced over at Dad. The dark outline of his face looked familiar. But I realized that I didn't know him anymore.

I broke the silence as we got off the bridge and onto the freeway. "Dad, I really don't want you to come. You'll just be interfering," I said.

"You're in over your head," Dad said. "You could be killed."

"But Darryl saved my life," I said. "I have to help him."

"Who's Darryl?" he asked.

I didn't answer.

Dad put his hand on my arm. "Give me a chance, Nick. Tell me what's going on."

So I did. I told him everything. As I talked, I remembered back to what happened at my apartment. How Darryl had killed the one alien. And how bad his charred remains smelled. Then I showed my dad Darryl's tube. "I have to get it back to him," I said. "Maybe he still has a chance to defeat his enemies."

"I want to help you," Dad said.

"Right." I didn't believe him.

After a long silence, he spoke. "You have to listen, Nick. I wanted to be there for you. And your mom."

"Then why weren't you?" I asked. It wasn't anger I was feeling now. It was sadness. I felt like crying.

"Listen to me," Dad said. "This is important. When my drinking got out of control, I lost everything. My job, the house, and you and Mom.

"And then my boss said he'd give me one more chance. If I joined a support group and quit drinking, I could have my job back. I've done that, Nick. And I've made a lot of progress. It's taken me two years."

"Are you cured?" I said.

"There is no cure. I'm recovering," he explained. "There are still times when I want a drink. Sometimes it's all I think about. But now I'm clean. I just want you to know that I never stopped thinking about you and Mom. But I was too ashamed to face either of you."

I thought back to when I was growing up. There were so many times when Dad came home drunk. Or he didn't come home at all. I saw what it was doing to my mother. She was always worried or crying. After a while,

I began to hate him. And I just wished he would die.

We were out in the country now. I could see the outline of the hills against the dark sky. The turnoff for Point Reyes would be coming up soon. I was feeling really tired by now. Dad offered to drive. I pulled over and we traded places.

Not long after we were back on the road, bright lights flooded the cab of the truck. There had been no other cars on the road. So we were both surprised. Then the lights started flashing.

"It's the police," Dad said. "Get in the backseat and lie down." Then he pulled over to the side of the road.

As I lie there, I could hear the crunch of gravel as the cop walked up to the truck.

"I need to see your ID and proof of insurance," the officer said.

"Sure," Dad said. "Was I speeding?"

The officer didn't answer. He was

studying Dad's ID. Finally he looked at Dad. "You don't have the proper license to be driving this vehicle," he said.

"Oh. Well, I can explain, Officer. I'm a plant manager for an electronics company. Able Electronics?" He unclipped the badge from his belt and showed it to him. "We had this urgent shipment for a hospital in the area. Some of their equipment failed. It was an emergency. So I'm helping out. But I can assure you that I've been properly trained to drive this truck."

The part about the hospital wasn't true. But was my loser dad really a manager?

There was a short, awkward pause while we waited for the officer's response.

"You must have missed all the excitement," the officer said. "Or have you heard? Your plant was destroyed a little earlier this afternoon."

"What?" Dad said, trying to sound shocked.

"Yeah. It's gone," he said. "Three people have been confirmed dead. And about a dozen were injured. They're still searching through the debris."

"I can't believe it," Dad said, shaking his head. "Do they know what caused it?"

"Not yet. But I hear they're looking at possible sabotage. Does the name Darryl sound familiar to you? Or the name Nick?" the officer asked. "Do you remember hearing about them being at the plant today?"

Dad was pretending to think about it. "No. I don't know anyone by those names," my dad lied.

"Okay," the officer said. Suddenly the bright beam of a flashlight was sweeping through the back of the truck. If the officer did a thorough search, he'd find me. But after a few moments, the flashlight clicked off. He handed Dad's ID and insurance card back to him.

"You know, you should have that license of yours updated," the officer said. "I can't promise you won't be fined the next time you're stopped."

Dad was nodding. "Understood, Officer. And thank you." He waited for the cop to get back into his car before starting the engine. Then Dad slowly drove away.

I started to get up, but Dad stopped me. "Stay there," he said. "I think he might follow us. I'm surprised he let me go."

"Do you think he knows more than he's letting on?" I asked.

"It's possible," Dad said.

At that point I started wondering how much information the cops actually had. Had they connected Darryl with the death at school? Had they spoken to Kara? Did they know anything about me?

Chapter 7

What are we going to do?" I asked my dad.

"That depends on how long this cop follows us. Hopefully it won't be all the way to Point Reyes."

As we drove, some memories of being at Point Reyes were coming back to me. We used to go there a lot as a family. Me and Mom and Dad. Mom would pack a lunch. We'd sit on a big blanket and eat. Then Mom would read or take a nap. Dad and I would run races along the water. He'd always let me win. Then he pretended he was going to throw me into the ocean.

◆ • ◆

After we'd been driving for an hour, I got back into the passenger seat. Dad said we were in the town of Point Reyes Station. It was about another forty minutes to the lighthouse.

"Do you think we're still being followed?" I asked.

"I'm not sure," he said. "I don't see a car behind us right now. But that cop could still be tailing us from a distance."

When we were about a mile from the lighthouse, Dad pulled into a parking lot. We would have to walk the rest of the way. There was a parking lot closer. But we didn't think it would be safe. That's when I saw headlights. A car was slowly coming up the road. "Let's go," I said. Before I got out of the truck, I shoved Darryl's tube into my pocket.

"Wait. I want to find something to use for protection," Dad said. He rummaged through a toolbox and pulled out a wrench. Then he got out of the truck and locked the doors.

I looked at the wrench in Dad's hand. "What good will that do us?" I asked.

"If nothing else, I can throw it at someone," Dad said. "Come on. Quick."

We ducked behind a large boulder and watched. The police car slowed as it got closer to the parking lot. But it didn't enter. If the cop was looking for us, it seems he would have turned in. Or maybe he knew we were there. But he was waiting to find out what we were up to.

We walked as quickly as we could, stumbling over low bushes and clumps of grass. At last we came to the edge of a steep cliff. Directly below was a narrow beach. We could see the historic lighthouse. It was no longer in operation. But a light was coming from a beacon on top of a nearby building. The light flashed every five seconds.

I put my hand on Dad's arm. "Quiet," I whispered. I thought I heard footsteps.

Suddenly a small herd of deer bounded past us and down the hill toward the beach.

Then powerful beams of light blinded us from two directions.

"Walk toward me," a voice said. "Keep your hands in front of you."

It was the cop who pulled Dad over. Another cop was there too. They walked us back to where the police cars were parked.

One of the cops spoke to me. He asked to see my ID. Then he told me he was going to take me in for questioning. It was regarding possible sabotage and a murder at the university. He read me my rights. And I was frisked from head to toe. It felt like I was having a bad dream.

At the same time I was being read my rights, the other cop was questioning my dad about the building explosion. Dad was refusing to talk.

Then I was put inside the police car. The metal screen between the front and back seats made me think of a cage. I felt a sense of panic.

What was going to happen to me and my dad? And what about Darryl? Now I wouldn't be able to help him. Then I thought of the tube in my pocket. I wished that I'd thrown it away. Maybe there was still a chance. "I need some water," I said to the cop. "Please, I feel sick."

The cop got out and opened the door to the backseat. He had a bottle of water in his hand. "Here," he said, handing it to me.

He was just about to close the door. Then another car moved toward us. As it moved slowly past, I saw Darryl's face. "There he is!" I called out. "Darryl is in that car!"

The other cop left my dad. He got into his car and took off, flashing his lights. Then he spoke into his loudspeaker. "This is the police. Pull over to the side of the road."

The car stopped. It hadn't gotten far. Dad walked over to me, and we watched the whole thing.

The cop pulled up behind the car. He got

out and drew his gun. The other cop left me and ran to assist. He was shouting to the people in the car. "Step out of the vehicle!" His gun was drawn.

They all did as he said. There were five of them altogether. It was the four aliens and Darryl. Everyone seemed calm. I didn't see the pole weapon anywhere.

"Hands in the air!" one cop shouted.

Just then, a rustle came from the darkness. The cops looked away for a split second. And in the next second, one of the aliens reached into his coat and pulled out the pole weapon. I could see it shining brightly in the headlights. Before the cops could do anything, a blinding light flooded over them. One of the aliens pushed Darryl into the car. Then the other three got in, and the car sped away.

Now it was silent. I didn't see the cops. Dad and I moved a little closer for a better look. There was nothing there but a large blackened hole where the cops had been standing. The smell of burned clothing filled the air.

Darryl would have said the two police officers had been destroyed. Was my friend destroyed too? I stood there feeling helpless.

Chapter 8

Let's follow them," Dad said.

"How are we going to do that?" I asked. "Walk there?"

"No," Dad said. "Let's take this." He was looking at the police car.

"You're joking, right? That has to be illegal."

"Nick," he said. "We couldn't be in more trouble if we tried."

We? Dad wasn't as involved in all of this as I was. I looked at him. "I guess we don't have much of a choice," I said. "Let's go."

Sitting in the front seat of a cop car didn't feel much better than sitting in the back. The dispatcher's voice kept coming on the radio. He was asking us to check in.

I knew it wouldn't be long before more cops showed up.

We drove up the hill to the visitors' center and parked. It would be a half-mile walk to the lighthouse. As we got out of the car, I noticed that it was unusually quiet. This place was known for its strong, howling winds. Especially this close to the water. Tonight it was just cold and foggy.

Dad and I climbed over the fence. Then we started down the steps leading to the lighthouse. There were just over three hundred. I knew that because once when I was a kid, I counted them.

At the bottom of the steps was the old lighthouse. Just below it was the light station. As the beacon flashed, I thought I saw something moving. And then I heard Darryl's whistle. "That's him," I said to Dad. "Darryl is either hurt or afraid."

We walked to the back of the light station. I quietly moved to the side of the building and peered around the corner. I wanted to get a look at what was going on. Then I saw the aliens. They were at the edge of the cliff, tying Darryl to a railing. One of Darryl's sleeves hung limp. It looked like he was missing an arm. His other hand clutched the backpack. Once Darryl was tied, the aliens searched the sky.

Dad and I also looked up. "There," I whispered.

It was a small revolving light glowing faintly through the fog. As the light turned, its rays seemed to flicker like a sparkling jewel.

One of the aliens was aiming the pole toward the sky. I wanted to scream. The pole had to be destroyed. But how?

At that moment light shot out from the weapon. The beam pierced the fog. And the jeweled light disappeared into the darkness. I saw Darryl close his eyes.

I had an idea. "Dad," I whispered. "Give

me a boost." For once he didn't question me. He helped me up onto the roof. Then I told him to hand me the wrench. I started to try to loosen the brackets that held the light in place. But they wouldn't budge.

Suddenly the whole roof lit up. "Police!" a voice said over a loudspeaker. "This is a warning. We're armed. You are advised to immediately come down from the roof."

When I looked up toward the voice, all that was visible were the silhouettes of several cops. Before Dad and I could respond, I heard something behind us. I turned and saw the little revolving light. It was still flickering like a jewel. It looked close enough to touch. Then there was a blast of white light. It shattered the jewel into a shower of fragments. I saw an alien. He was aiming the pole at Darryl.

"No!" I yelled.

But another bolt of light shot from the pole, and the backpack melted. In that second, I saw a mist of colors and a thousand eyes. Then the eyes closed. And there was nothing. Darryl's hope of a new life for his people had come to an end. And Darryl, whose head was dropped forward, looked like he was dead too.

Chapter 9

It's loose!" Dad said.

I turned and stared in disbelief. Dad had managed to loosen the light. I swiveled it to focus the beam toward the cliff. The aliens' faces looked stark white in the intense light. I could see them staring at me. One of them raised the pole.

I pulled Darryl's tube from my pocket and held it in front of the light. A thousand watts of power poured through the tube and hit the cliff like a rocket. Each of the aliens was caught in his own cocoon of fiery light. Then the brilliant cocoons went black. Only ragged pieces of scorched clothing remained as they drifted in the sky.

I jumped down from the roof and ran

to Darryl. Dad was right behind me. We untied Darryl, and slowly he lifted his head. His eyes were open.

"Darryl! You're alive," I said. "But your arm. What happened to it?" I asked.

"My arm and I broke up. Just like your mother and father," he said, trying to smile. "I knew you would come, Nick. Do you have the container I gave you?"

That's right! The container. I'd forgotten about it. There was still hope after all. "Yes!" I said. I took it out of my pocket and placed it in his hand. When I closed his fingers over it, I felt a mild shock.

His eyes glowed. "I was right about you. I knew you were the one," he said.

Darryl looked up at the sky. Dad and I looked too. Peeping through the fog was another jeweled light. It was coming closer and closer. If I reached out, I could have touched it. Then the light grew very bright and started to pulse in different colors.

The container in Darryl's hand opened. Inside there were two pairs of eyes. They rose up and were absorbed by the pulsating colors. Then the colors became a single white light again. And it disappeared.

In time, the eyes would multiply and be ready to grow. Just like the thousand eyes Darryl had tried so hard to protect but in the end couldn't. The hope he'd had for his planet to be created again would now be realized. Darryl had sacrificed everything to make sure it would happen.

I looked at my alien friend. His face was peaceful. But I could see that he had aged. He looked very old. And now he was no longer alive. I turned away as I fought the tears.

Dad and I waited for the cops at the base of the steps. They asked us a few questions, then escorted us back up to a police car. Soon we were headed for San Francisco. On the way I wondered how we were going to explain everything without sounding crazy. It was going to be a long night. But it had all been worth it. And I was sure that someday Dad and I would look back and laugh.

But as we got farther from Point Reyes, I felt a mix of emotions. I was *the one*, as Darryl had said. That made me feel good. I hadn't let him down. But I also felt sad that I'd lost my friend.

And how wrong I'd been about knowing people. Some expert judge I was. There was Darryl, who I thought was going to be self-centered and sneaky. He turned out to be a hero. But Kara hadn't been cool at all. And I thought my dad was a hopeless loser. But he'd overcome so much in his life. Now he was doing well. I was proud to be his son. I leaned my head back and shut my eyes. Tonight I would dream about the jewel-colored lights.

Comprehension Questions

Recall

1. What was Nick's first impression of Darryl's personality?

2. When they burst into Nick's room, who did the enemy aliens pretend to be?

3. In what strange way did Darryl eat his food?

Analyzing Characters

1. What two words could describe Nick?
   - *courageous*
   - *spiteful*
   - *faithful*

2. What two words could describe Darryl?
   - *boring*
   - *desperate*
   - *unusual*

3. What two words could describe Kara?
   - *resourceful*

- *ruthless*
- *suspicious*

4. What two words could describe Nick's dad?
   - *critical*
   - *regretful*
   - *helpful*

Who and Where?

1. Where were Darryl and Nick when Darryl first used his tube?

2. Where were Nick and Darryl when the police started chasing them?

Drawing Conclusions

1. What was in Darryl's backpack?

2. What conclusion did Darryl draw about the tiny insect on the bus?